# Felicia
## the Fidget Toy
## Fairy

Join the **Rainbow Magic Reading Challenge!**

Read the story and collect your fairy points to climb the Reading Rainbow at the back of the book.

This book is worth 1 star.

# To Katelyn, wishing you a magical future

## Special thanks to
## Rachel Elliot

ORCHARD BOOKS

First published in Great Britain in 2023 by Hodder & Stoughton
1 3 5 7 9 10 8 6 4 2

© 2023 Rainbow Magic Limited.
© 2023 HIT Entertainment Limited.
Illustrations © 2023 Hodder & Stoughton Limited.

A CIP catalogue record for this book is available from the British Library.

ISBN 978 1 40836 991 3

Printed and bound in Great Britain by Clays Ltd, Elcograf S.p.A.

MIX
Paper from
responsible sources
FSC® C104740

The paper and board used in this book are made from wood from responsible sources

Orchard Books
An imprint of Hachette Children's Group
Part of Hodder & Stoughton Limited
Carmelite House, 50 Victoria Embankment, London EC4Y 0DZ

An Hachette UK Company
www.hachette.co.uk
www.hachettechildrens.co.uk

# Felicia
## the Fidget Toy Fairy

### By Daisy Meadows

ORCHARD

www.orchardseriesbooks.co.uk

# Jack Frost's Spell

I want my servants to obey,
And wait upon me night and day.
To rush to do each little task,
Surely it's not too much to ask!

They fuss and fidget all day long,
And get the simplest mischief wrong.
But with the toys I steal today,
They'll focus on each word I say!

# Contents

# Chapter One
# Happy New Year

Rachel Walker shivered. The biting January wind was making her face tingle. She pulled her woolly hat down over her ears and dashed through the school gate. No one was lingering in the playground this morning.

Her friends Kayla and Millie were

hanging up their coats in the cloakroom.

"Morning," said Rachel. "Happy New Year!"

It was their first day back at school after the Christmas holiday. Everyone was talking at the same time, comparing presents and chatting about where they had gone and who they had seen. Rachel smiled as she hung her coat on her peg. She and her best friend, Kirsty Tate, had shared another magical adventure in Fairyland. Luckily, none of her classmates had ever guessed that she was secretly friends with the fairies.

"I wonder what the new teacher will be like," said Millie, shaking her curly hair out of her eyes.

"I wish Mr Beaker hadn't left," said Rachel. "I hope the new teacher is nice."

"Me too," said Kayla. "I heard that—"

She broke off as their classmate Tom burst into the cloakroom and barged Millie out of the way.

"I slid on every iced-over puddle all the way to school, and there were twenty-three, and I was like the best ice skater ever—" he threw his coat and bag on the floor, "and I got a new computer game for Christmas, and I'm already at level four, and—"

He skidded out of the cloakroom again, knocking Kayla's water bottle out of her hand. It landed on her foot and she yelped.

"Ouch," she cried out. "I wish Tom would learn to slow down and be calm. He does everything at ten miles a minute."

"It's really distracting," Millie agreed.

"Mr Beaker said he finds it hard to concentrate," Rachel reminded them. "He said we all need to be understanding, because Tom can't help it."

In the classroom, Tom was loudly telling everyone about how he had reached level four of his new game. Rachel sat down as the new teacher clapped her hands and asked for silence.

"Good morning, class," she said warmly.

"My name is Mrs Ratha, and I am looking forward to getting to know you all over the next few months."

Rachel liked her at once. Her face was kind and she was tall, with brown hair and sparkling eyes.

"I am sure that you must all be missing Mr Beaker, but I hope that we can share our excitement about learning and have a wonderful year together." She bent down and lifted a box on to her desk. "This is something I used in my old

school," she went on, "and I hope it will work well here too. I call it a fidget box. It is filled with objects that help children who find it hard to concentrate."

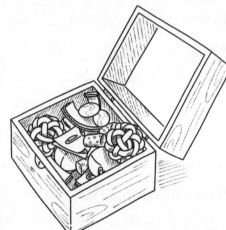

"What sort of objects?" asked Kayla at once.

Mrs Ratha smiled and peeped into the box.

"Let me see," she replied. "I have tangle balls, sticky tack, paperclips, corks, stress balls, smooth stones, velcro . . . and a few surprises."

"How will they help us?" asked Jessy.

"Fidget toys give your hands something to do so that your brain can get on with listening and learning," said Mrs Ratha.

"Anyone can collect a toy for the lesson. After all, it must be a bit stressful getting a brand-new teacher."

A few children got up to choose a toy, including Rachel. She was usually good at concentrating, but today a little extra help would be nice. Even though Mrs Ratha seemed nice, it was strange not to see Mr Beaker. She and Tom picked a fidget popper out at the same time.

"I'm going to start with a bit of general knowledge," said Mrs Ratha, a smile flitting around her mouth. "I think that a few fun facts will start this term in the right way."

Mrs Ratha taught them lots of funny things about animals, history, science and art. It was a hilarious lesson and Rachel found it easy to concentrate playing

with the fidget popper while she listened. Just when everyone thought that they couldn't giggle any more, Mrs Ratha mentioned that gorillas burp when they are happy, and the whole class fell to pieces again. No one wanted the lesson to end.

Breaktime arrived, and the children put their fidget toys back in the box and ran outside to play. Rachel heard Tom telling some Year Fours that pigs can't look up into the sky and kangaroos can't jump backwards.

"The fidget popper must have really helped Tom to concentrate," she said to Millie and Kayla. "He's learned loads."

But as soon as break ended and they got back into the classroom, it was clear that something was wrong. Mrs Ratha looked extremely serious.

"I'm afraid that something unpleasant has happened," she said. "While we were all out of the classroom, someone must have sneaked in. Every single fidget toy is missing!"

## Chapter Two
# A Secret in the Cupboard

No one could imagine where the fidget toys had gone. Why would someone have taken them, and who would do anything so mean?

"Rachel, please go to my supplies cupboard and fetch the blue bag from the table," said Mrs Ratha. "I have some spare toys in there."

Rachel went willingly into the supplies cupboard at the back of the classroom. She always loved the chance to see the neat rows of coloured exercise books, boxes of pens, fresh glue sticks and carefully labelled tubs of craft supplies.

Everything looked just the same as when it had been Mr Beaker's cupboard, except for a blue bag that was lying on the floor.

"That must be the one," Rachel said to herself.

She picked it up, but it was as light as a feather. Had these toys been stolen too? Rachel turned the bag upside down and shook it, just in case. A tiny fidget spinner fell out and rolled across the floor. Rachel grabbed for it, but it darted sideways out of her reach.

"Hey!" she said, "Come back here."

The little toy rolled all the way around the edge of the tiny supplies cupboard. Rachel chased it, but every time she tried to pick it up, it changed direction and escaped her.

"OK," said Rachel to herself. "This is seriously weird."

She stopped and stared at the spinner. It stopped rolling and twirled around like a spinning coin. Now it was still, Rachel

could see that it had a faint, silvery glow. The fidget spinner bounced into the air and then, with a puff of silvery fairy dust, turned into a tiny fairy.

"It's magical to meet you," she said, waving both her hands and beaming with smiles. "I'm Felicia the Fidget Toy Fairy."

"Hi, Felicia," said

Rachel, kneeling down. "What a lovely surprise."

Felicia fluttered down and perched on Rachel's knee. She was wearing a flower-print T-shirt, blue shorts and white trainers, and her dark brown hair was braided into tiny, beaded plaits all over her head. Rachel noticed that she was fiddling with some of the beads at the end of a plait.

"I've come to ask for your help," she said. "Lots of people need fidget toys to help them focus, including me. That's why Queen Titania gave me this job. I make sure that each person gets the perfect fidget toy for them."

"I used one this morning," said Rachel. "It really helped. How do you know what each person needs?"

"I have a magical fidget popper,"
Felicia explained. "It helps me to guide
each person to the best fidget toy for
them, and to make sure there are enough
toys to go around. At least, it did help me
do those things, until this morning."

"What happened this morning?"
Rachel asked.

"I live in a big soft-play castle called
the Fidget Fort," said Felicia. "It's the
coolest house ever, and I love it. Anyone
is welcome to come in and enjoy it with
me. This morning some goblins came to
play . . . and one of them left with my
special rainbow fidget popper."

"I bet Jack Frost sent them to spoil
things for everyone else," Rachel
exclaimed.

"That's what I thought," said Felicia.

"Will you and Kirsty help me to get my popper back?"

"Of course we will," said Rachel at once. "But Kirsty goes to a different school."

Felicia gave a little wink.

"That's OK," she said. "The queen has given me special permission to magic Kirsty out of her school too. We'll see her in Fairyland."

"It's lucky that I'm on my own in here," said Rachel, jumping to her feet. "No one will see me transform."

She knew that time would stand still in the human world while she was in Fairyland.

Felicia fluttered into the air and waved her wand. A shower of tiny flowers sprinkled down on Rachel, bursting into

fairy dust as they touched her. She shrank to fairy size and shimmering wings glistened on her back. Felicia took her hand.

"Let's go," she said.

She waved her wand around them, wrapping them in sparkling coils of golden light. Then the coils unwound, sending them spinning through a blue sky, past white clouds like marshmallow puffs.

"Hello, Fairyland," Rachel called out, laughing as she fluttered her wings and followed Felicia downwards. "It's good to be back!"

## Chapter Three
## The Fidget Fort

Felicia landed lightly beside the biggest, brightest soft-play that Rachel had ever seen. It was huge!

"This must be almost three times as big as my house!" Rachel exclaimed.

Felicia laughed and clapped her hands, looking at Rachel's amazed face.

"You like it?" she said. "Everyone here loves the Fidget Fort. It's my favourite place in Fairyland."

Before Rachel could reply, there was a distant whooshing sound and a squeal of laughter, and then Kirsty appeared in a flurry of fairy dust.

"Best surprise ever!" she said as soon as she saw Rachel. "One minute I was pond-dipping for newts, and the next I was the size of a newt."

The best friends hugged and then Rachel quickly explained why they were there.

"It's great to meet you, Felicia," said Kirsty. "Of course we'll help."

Felicia led them into the Fidget Fort.

"Every day, fairies and goblins come here to relax," she said. "But today I have

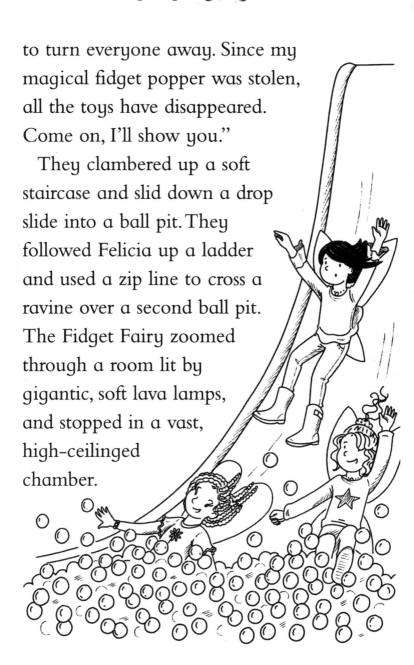

to turn everyone away. Since my magical fidget popper was stolen, all the toys have disappeared. Come on, I'll show you."

They clambered up a soft staircase and slid down a drop slide into a ball pit. They followed Felicia up a ladder and used a zip line to cross a ravine over a second ball pit. The Fidget Fairy zoomed through a room lit by gigantic, soft lava lamps, and stopped in a vast, high-ceilinged chamber.

"This is really your home?" asked Kirsty in wonder.

"Yes, and my playground too," said Felicia.

"It makes me feel happy just being here," said Rachel.

"This is the main playroom," said Felicia, smiling at them.

Rachel and Kirsty saw squashy tables and chairs, life-size games of chess and skittles, a climbing wall, a soft pirate ship and gigantic see-through balls that they could climb inside. Mesh hanging storage bags dangled from the ceiling, but they were all empty.

"Usually, these are filled with fidget toys," said Felicia. "I keep every size, colour and type, so everyone can find one they love. But after my magical

popper was stolen, they all disappeared.
Come into the viewing room."

She led Rachel and Kirsty into a
smaller side room.

"What's that?" asked Kirsty.

She pointed at a red ribbon that was
hanging from the ceiling.

"That's where I keep my magical fidget
popper," said Felicia. "It always hangs
there, so that everyone can enjoy using
it. Just one pop can make anyone feel
calmer."

One of the walls looked like a mirror,
but it wasn't made of glass. Rachel
reached out a hand. It felt shiny and soft,
like silk.

"It reflects anything that has happened
in this room," said Felicia. "Look at what
happened this morning."

She waved her wand and the mirrored wall shimmered into a screen. The viewing room in the reflection looked very different. It was filled with fidget toys, and a rainbow-coloured fidget popper was dangling from the red ribbon. A group of goblins was playing leapfrog and making a loud racket of squawks and cackles.

"Let's go and see the ball pit," one of them shouted.

They all ran out, and for a moment the room was empty. Then a small goblin crept back in, looking over his shoulder. When he was sure that no one was watching, he yanked the beautiful fidget popper down from the ribbon and ran out with it.

"He's bound to be following Jack Frost's

orders," said Kirsty at once. "He's been sent to spoil things for everyone else. Don't worry, Felicia. We'll get your magical popper back and everything will be OK again."

Felicia was fiddling with the beads in her hair again.

"Now you two are here, I'm sure everything's going to be all right," she said. "Let's find Jack Frost and make him give back my magical popper."

Rachel and Kirsty exchanged a knowing look. They had faced Jack Frost many times, and they knew that it was impossible to make him do anything.

"Let's find out where the magical fidget popper is first," Kirsty suggested. "Maybe we can find a way into the Ice Castle and look around without being seen."

Felicia reached out her free hand, and Rachel and Kirsty layered their hands on top. Then Felicia tapped the hands with her wand, sprinkling them with golden fairy dust.

"Teamwork," she said. "This spell will keep us warm among the ice and snow."

Feeling as if they were glowing from the inside out, the fairies zoomed into the air and headed towards Jack Frost's freezing corner of Fairyland. Before long, the toadstool houses and sunny little gardens were behind them. Soon they were fluttering in the shadow of the Ice Castle's grim turrets.

"We have to find a way in that isn't guarded," said Rachel.

But Kirsty shook her head.

"I think we should explore outside first," she said. "Look!"

Jack Frost was standing in the castle gardens in front of a group of young goblins.

# Chapter Four
# Goblins in Training

The fairies flew out of sight behind a holly bush and watched. Jack Frost had a large flip chart on an easel. A group of young goblins was sitting in front of him on the frozen grass, and he was pointing to the chart with his wand.

"I think he's teaching them," said

Rachel in amazement. "Goodness, those poor goblins. I'm glad he's not my teacher."

The heading on the flip chart read *How to be a Good Servant to Jack Frost*. He had written a long list of rules.

Obey me
Listen to me
Make me sandwiches
Laugh at all my jokes
Steal from the fairies
Never argue with me
Tell me how brilliant I am all day long
Agree with everything I say
Be naughty
Don't fidget

"This is terrible advice," said Felicia,

fiddling with her plait. "A good leader asks for the opposite of all those things."

"Stop fidgeting, pea-brain!" Jack Frost bellowed at a goblin in the back row.

The goblin jumped as if he had been jabbed by a bolt of blue lightning.

"It was my fault, Your Iciness," piped up a smaller goblin beside him. "I distracted him."

"Then you're both pea-brains and will be punished," Jack Frost yelled.

"I can't bear another moment of this," exclaimed Felicia.

"Maybe we should just—" Kirsty began.

But Felicia had already scrambled out of their hiding place and was boldly walking up to the Ice Lord. Rachel and Kirsty hurried to catch up with her. Jack

Frost was staring at her in disbelief.

"How dare you come to my castle?" he roared.

"We'd be glad to go home," said Felicia. "Just give me back what you have stolen."

"Stolen?" Jack Frost exclaimed in an outraged tone. "What an insult!"

He shuffled sideways to hide his chart from view.

"Give me my magical fidget popper," said Felicia, holding out her hand.

Jack Frost was staring at her with a

completely puzzled expression.

"I don't know anything about fidget poppers," he said. "Clear off."

Kirsty noticed something move out of the corner of her eye. She turned, just in time to see the two goblins from the back row slipping out of sight behind a frozen bush.

"I know you sent a goblin to take it," Felicia went on.

"I haven't got time for your boring toys," Jack Frost retorted. "I'm far too busy teaching these chumps how to look after me properly. You've ruined my lesson. Clear off back to your puny pink palace. Go away."

Rachel gently pulled Felicia's hand.

"Come on," she said.

They turned and walked away, feeling

puzzled. Jack Frost was never usually shy about owning up to his mischief. In fact, he normally enjoyed gloating about it.

"Why is he lying?" asked Felicia.

"Maybe he's not," said Kirsty.

She had spotted one of the bushes rustling. Remembering the goblins who had hidden, she parted the bush and saw them crouching down inside.

"Oh, I know you," said Felicia to the littlest goblin. "You're the one who took my popper!"

"They're scared," said Rachel, noticing the two goblin's fearful expressions.

"I don't think Jack Frost knows what they did," said Kirsty.

The goblins were trembling from their pointy ears to the tips of their large toes. Felicia gave them her kindest smile.

"Please don't be afraid," she said. "I forgive you and you're not in trouble, but I must have the popper back."

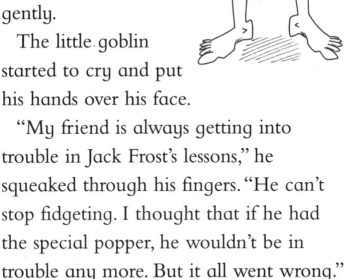

"Why did you take it?" asked Kirsty, gently.

The little goblin started to cry and put his hands over his face.

"My friend is always getting into trouble in Jack Frost's lessons," he squeaked through his fingers. "He can't stop fidgeting. I thought that if he had the special popper, he wouldn't be in trouble any more. But it all went wrong."

He threw back his head and wailed.

The fairies patted him on the back, and Felicia produced a clean handkerchief. The goblin blew his nose into it loudly.

"When I took the popper back to Goblin Grotto," he went on, "all sorts of other fidget toys started arriving. My hut is filled with them, and they're spilling into the streets. Everyone in Goblin Grotto is furious with me."

Felicia gave him a sympathetic smile.

"You were trying to be kind," she said. "But doing the wrong thing for the right reasons doesn't make it OK. It is wrong to steal.

"I'm sorry," said the goblin, hanging his head.

"What an unusual goblin," murmured Rachel to Kirsty and Felicia.

"Not really," said Felicia. "Goblins are

 **Goblins in Training**

taught how to be naughty by Jack Frost.
It seems as if our friend here isn't very
good at his lessons."

"He was doing it for me," said the other
goblin. "We're best friends for ever."

"I have an idea," said Felicia. "If you
take me to your home in Goblin Grotto,
I'll clean up all the toys in a twinkling.
Then I'll make a special fidget toy just
for your friend."

The young goblins nodded eagerly, and
Rachel and Kirsty shared a smile.

"I love a happy ending," said Rachel.

"Me too," said Kirsty. "And for once,
Jack Frost has nothing to do with it."

"Think again!" said a nasty voice, and
they all spun around as a cackling laugh
filled the air.

Jack Frost had heard every single word.

## Chapter Five
# The Tower of Toys

Jack Frost was staring at the smallest goblin.

"Well done, pea-brain," he said. "You've caused a lot of trouble in the human world. You'll be a great mischief maker."

The little goblin beamed with pride.

He pointed his wand into the grey sky

and it released a streak of blue lightning.

"All the fidget toys have now been moved to my castle," he went on, "and that is where they will stay. The human world will become a more anxious, stressful place, and you can do nothing about it. Ha ha!"

He turned his back on them, and his cloak swirled around him.

"Follow me, goblins!" he ordered.

The little goblin jumped up and started to follow his master, but his friend didn't move.

"What are you waiting for?" said the little goblin, pausing.

"He's scared," said Rachel. "If Felicia can't make him that special fidget toy, he'll keep getting into trouble with Jack Frost."

The goblin stared at her, and then at his friend. He looked at the disappearing figure of Jack Frost, and then let out a long sigh. He came back and put his arm around his friend's shoulders.

"How can I help?" he asked,

"I just need the magical rainbow fidget popper that you took," said Felicia. "I can put everything right if I have that."

Looking scared, the goblin nodded.

"It must be in the castle somewhere," he said. Jack Frost will have guards on every door, but I'll try to find a way in for you."

The goblins raced towards the castle, and the fairies waited anxiously outside. The gardens seemed very quiet under their blanket of snow.

"It's strange to be trusting a goblin to

help us," said Felicia, playing with one of her plaits. "I hope we're not making a mistake."

"I believe in him," said Kirsty.

"Me too," said Rachel.

A few minutes passed, and then they heard a window squeak open high above them. The goblin leaned out and beckoned.

"Quickly," he hissed.

The fairies zoomed upwards and in through the open window. They were standing in a dark corridor. Rachel felt an icy drip run down her back and looked up. Icicles were clinging to the ceiling.

"I really don't like this place," she whispered.

"He's probably put the toys in one of

the towers," said the goblin. "Come on."

He ran ahead of them through freezing corridors and stopped at the bottom of a winding staircase. Toys were spilling down the steps. Rachel saw fidget spinners, poppers shaped like animals and sweets, fidget tangles, smooth pebbles, pots of sticky slime, squishy animals, chew sticks, stretchy people, twisty tubes, slinkies,

puzzle cubes, stretch noodles and many more toys that she had never seen before.

"There must be thousands of fidget toys crammed into this tower," said Felicia in despair. "How can we find the magical fidget popper among all these? It's impossible!"

# Chapter Six
# Happy Fidgeting

"I don't like the word 'impossible'," said Kirsty in a determined voice.

Rachel grinned at her.

"I know that look," she said. "You've got an idea, haven't you?

"Yes," Kirsty replied. "Felicia, I know that your rainbow fidget popper will

glow with fairy magic. Is there a spell
that will make the glow brighter? Maybe
that will help us to find the toy."

"That's a great idea!" Felicia exclaimed.
"And I know just the spell."

She lifted her wand and pointed it into
the mound of toys.

"Fairy magic, brightly shine,
Guide me to the toy that's mine."

A fountain of fairy dust erupted from
her wand tip, sprinkling the fidget toys
with sparkling light and disappearing
into every nook and cranny. The light
faded, and for a long time nothing
happened. Then—

"Look," said Rachel in a half whisper.
"I can see something."

A faint glow had appeared, deep in the pile of toys. The fairies started to dig the toys out of the way, but there were shouts and yells ringing around the castle.

"They know we're here," said Kirsty, panting. "Dig faster!"

They plunged deeper and deeper into the piles of fidget toys. Spinners, poppers, clickers, squishies and tangles flew into

the air around them. Running footsteps were behind them, and then goblins flung themselves into the pile, squawking and scrabbling past the fairies.

"Find me that popper," Jack Frost's voice bellowed behind them. "And stop those pesky fairies!"

Rachel's heart lurched. A glimmering rainbow popper was glowing brightly just ahead of her. She stretched out her arm to its fullest reach, but her fingertips only brushed it.

"Just . . . a little . . . more," she whispered, straining her arm.

Then she had a wonderful piece of luck. A goblin rammed into her, shoving her forwards, and her hand closed around the popper.

"Yes!" she exclaimed. "Felicia, here."

She threw it towards Felicia, who flew forward and caught it. Clutching her fidget popper close to her chest, she waved her wand. The heaps of toys vanished, and fairies and goblins tumbled to the ice-cold floor.

"The toys are back where they belong," said Felicia.

"You interfering fairies!" Jack Frost roared. "You'll be sorry for this. The goblins I'm training now will help me get my revenge."

He had no idea that the littlest goblin

had helped them. Felicia winked at the goblin and gave the tiniest flick of her wand. A tiny green fidget spinner appeared in his hand for his friend.

"Get them!" shouted Jack Frost.

The goblins scrambled to their feet and lurched towards the fairies.

"I think it's time for us to go," said Kirsty hastily.

They zoomed up the winding staircase and darted out through the first window they saw. Hovering outside the castle, they saw the goblins hanging out of the window, snatching at the air.

"Goodbye!" called Rachel, waving her hand.

She hoped that the little goblin would know that she was waving to him.

The fairies flew faster than arrows until they reached the green fields of Fairyland. Felicia slowed and fluttered down beside a lazy little stream, which was splashing and tinkling in the sunshine.

"Thank you," she said, hugging them warmly. "You saved me today, and you saved everyone who uses fidget toys."

"You saved that goblin and his friend," Kirsty replied, smiling. "I think we all did good work today."

Felicia raised her wand.

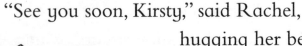

"It's time for me to send you back to your schools," she said. "But will you come back at the weekend for a play in the Fidget Fort?"

"We'd love to," said Rachel and Kirsty together.

Felicia smiled and waved her wand. Fairy dust began to whirl around them.

"See you soon, Kirsty," said Rachel,

hugging her best friend.

Then the magic whisked her away, and Rachel was standing in the supplies cupboard once more. No time had passed in the human world, so it was still empty. Only one thing had changed; the blue bag was full of fidget toys.

"Yes!" said Rachel to herself.

She took the bag back to her classroom, where Mrs Ratha was looking much happier.

"The fidget box is full again," she told Rachel. "I can't understand what happened. But the main thing is that all the toys have been returned."

Millie and Kayla were rummaging in the box. As Rachel watched, they pulled out the fidget popper that Tom had been using earlier.

"Here you are, Tom," said Millie, giving him the popper.

"Thanks," said Tom, looking surprised. "This really helped."

"We know," said Kayla, kindly. "It's important to use tools that make things a bit easier."

Rachel smiled and gently rubbed the necklace that Queen Titania had given her. She knew that miles away in Wetherbury, Kirsty was doing the same thing, thinking of their trip to Fairyland at the weekend.

"Mrs Ratha's pretty cool, isn't she?" said Kayla.

"Yes," said Rachel. "And I have a feeling that she's going to be a magical teacher!"

The End

# Meet Gracie and Khadijah, Fairyland's newest friends!

Find out how they discover the magic secret in Hope the Welcome Fairy!

Now it's time for Kirsty, Rachel,
Gracie and Khadijah to help ...

# Hope the Welcome Fairy

**Read on for a sneak peek ...**

Leaning out of her bedroom window,
Gracie Adebayo watched the removal
van driving away. She felt a tingle of
excitement. She already loved her new
room.

"I hope you like me, Wetherbury," she
whispered. "And I hope I like you!"

Gracie and her mums had moved
into one of the newly built houses in
Hawthorn Grove. Everything here was
fresh and new, from her new bedroom
to the park across the street. It was very
different from their old flat in the city
centre.

Her parents came in carrying more boxes. As usual, her mum looked graceful, her black bob sleek and shiny. Her mama had several smears of paint on her face and three pegs in her curly red hair. Gracie grinned at them both.

"I think these boxes are yours," said her mum, playing with one of Gracie's braids. "There is a lot to unpack."

"I'll start now," said Gracie eagerly, opening the nearest box. "Oh – paintbrushes."

"Oops, that box should be in my art studio," said her mama.

They went out, and Gracie was about to open a box when something caught her eye.

Through her bedroom window, she could see her next-door neighbours' house. A girl was standing at the window. Her dark brown hair hung in two long plaits, and she was resting her chin on her hands as she stared up into the sky.

Gracie opened her window.

"Hi," she called out.

The girl smiled.

"Doesn't the sky look huge?" she said. "In the city there were always buildings between me and the sky. Here, I feel as if I could just grow wings and zoom into it."

"I came from a city too," said Gracie. "I'm Gracie Adebayo."

"I'm Khadijah Khan," said the girl. "I was hoping that another child would live nearby."

"Same here," said Gracie, smiling.

A garland of brightly coloured bunting was hanging in Khadijah's window.

"I like your decorations," said Gracie. "They remind me of ship's flags. Did you know that sailors use flags to send messages to other ships?"

Khadijah's eyes sparkled with excitement.

"I've had an idea!" she exclaimed. "I'll give you some of my bunting, and we can put messages in our windows."

Gracie felt a rush of happiness. She hadn't even been here for a whole day yet, and she had already made a friend.

"I love that idea," she called across to Khadijah. "Let's say blue means 'good morning' and pink means 'good night'."

"Yes!" Khadijah replied happily. "There's a gap in the fence between our two gardens so yellow could mean 'meet me in the garden'. Let's call it our rainbow signal."

Suddenly, a tiny, glowing shape whizzed between their houses and disappeared into the park opposite. Khadijah gasped and Gracie's heart quickened. There had been something rather unusual about the shape.

"What was that?" Khadijah exclaimed.

"Let's find out," said Gracie. "Come on!"

When Gracie had checked with her mums and dashed outside, Khadijah was already waiting at her front gate.

"Did your parents say yes?" asked Gracie.

"Not just my parents," said Khadijah with a smile. "Also my aunt, my uncle, and my grandparents. Grandad's the only one who never tells me what to do."

"It must be fun to have such a big family," said Gracie. "In our house it's just me and my mums."

"Do you like your new house?"
Khadijah asked.

"Definitely," said Gracie with a smile.
"I'm a bit nervous about starting school,
though."

Khadijah gave her a questioning look.

"Every time I meet new people I
have to explain that I was born without
my left hand." Gracie told her. "Other
children usually ask questions, and it's not
always easy to answer them."

"It must be hard," said Khadijah. "But
I'll be with you, so you won't be alone.
I have a feeling that we're going to be
good friends."

The girls shared a smile and crossed the
road.

"There's going to be a street party here tomorrow," said Khadijah. "Everyone in Wetherbury is coming to meet everyone in Hawthorn Grove."

"Great idea," said Gracie. "I love parties."

"My dad helped to organise it," said Khadijah, pushing open the yellow park gate. "OK, where did that glowing thing land?"

The park was bright and shiny. There was a yellow climbing frame with ladders, rope bridges, a slide and a sliding pole. There was a set of red swings, a green seesaw and a zip line, as well as a trampoline built into the ground, a purple roundabout and a rainbow-coloured climbing wall. A weeping willow stood at the back of the park, surrounded by bushes. Its branches grazed the grass.

Gracie and Khadijah checked behind the bushes, around the equipment and even up in the tree. But the glowing shape had vanished.

"Never mind," said Khadijah. "Let's play."

Just then, Gracie heard a faint, silvery giggle. She turned, trying to follow the sound.

"What is it?" asked Khadijah.

Gracie shrugged.

"I thought I heard something . . ."

They both listened, but the only sounds were the birds twittering and the leaves rustling in the breeze.

"Want to try the zip line?" Khadijah asked.

The girls clambered on together and

squealed with excitement as they whizzed along the wire. They bumped to a halt, giggling and breathless.

"Best fun ever!" said Khadijah.

Just then, two older girls walked in to the park. The first had blonde, wavy hair, and the other's dark hair was tucked behind her ears. They had matching gold lockets.

"Hi," said the blonde girl. "Isn't this park amazing?"

"Yes, we love it," said Khadijah. "Have you moved in to Hawthorn Grove too?"

"No, I'm here visiting my best friend," said the girl. "I'm Rachel Walker and this is Kirsty Tate."

Gracie liked them at once.

"I'm Gracie Adebayo, and this is Khadijah Khan," she said. "We've just arrived."

"Welcome to Wetherbury," said Kirsty, with a warm smile. "I love it here. Are you going to the street party tomorrow?"

"Definitely," said Khadijah, pulling herself on to the climbing frame. "Come on, let's play!"

Read *Hope the Welcome Fairy* to find out what adventures are in store for Kirsty, Rachel, Gracie and Khadijah!

**Calling all parents, carers and teachers!**
The Rainbow Magic fairies are here to help
your child enter the magical world of reading.
Whatever reading stage they are at, there's
a Rainbow Magic book for everyone!
Here is Lydia the Reading Fairy's guide to
supporting your child's journey at all levels.

## Starting Out

Our Rainbow Magic Beginner Readers are perfect for first-time readers who are just beginning to develop reading skills and confidence. Approved by teachers, they contain a full range of educational levelling, as well as lively full-colour illustrations.

## Developing Readers

Rainbow Magic Early Readers contain longer stories and wider vocabulary for building stamina and growing confidence. These are adaptations of our most popular Rainbow Magic stories, specially developed for younger readers in conjunction with an Early Years reading consultant, with full-colour illustrations.

## Going Solo

The Rainbow Magic chapter books – a mixture of series and one-off specials – contain accessible writing to encourage your child to venture into reading independently. These highly collectible and much-loved magical stories inspire a love of reading to last a lifetime.

www.orchardseriesbooks.co.uk

"Rainbow Magic got my daughter reading chapter books. Great sparkly covers, cute fairies and traditional stories full of magic that she found impossible to put down" – Mother of Edie (6 years)

"Florence LOVES the Rainbow Magic books. She really enjoys reading now" – Mother of Florence (6 years)

# Read along the Reading Rainbow!

**Well done – you have completed the book!**

This book was worth 1 star.

See how far you have climbed on the Reading Rainbow opposite.
The more books you read, the more stars you can colour in
and the closer you will be to becoming a Royal Fairy!

**Do you want to print your own Reading Rainbow?**

1) Go to the Rainbow Magic website

2) Download and print out the poster

3) Colour in a star for every book you finish
and climb the Reading Rainbow

4) For every step up the rainbow,
you can download your very own certificate

# There's all this and lots more at
## orchardseriesbooks.co.uk

You'll find activities, stories, a special newsletter
AND you can search for the fairy with your name!